Jo-anne Hawke
491 Dunn Street
Tor. Ontario
M6S-3G8

# THE MARIGOLD LINE

# THE
# Marigold Line

## CHARLES GRIFFITHS

## Collins
### LONDON AND GLASGOW

First printed in this edition 1970

ISBN 0 00 164230 8

© *Wm. Collins Sons & Co. Ltd.*

PRINTED AND MADE IN GREAT BRITAIN BY
WM. COLLINS SONS AND CO. LTD.
LONDON AND GLASGOW

# CONTENTS

# ILLUSTRATIONS

This book
is for all railway loving cats and kittens,
but especially for
"Mac", Jumbo
and
Miss Shani, the Siamese,
and her class of thirty happy kittens.

May they have many happy picnics
with Mr. Marmalade and his friends
on
*The Marigold Special*

## 1 *The problem must be solved*

Something tremendously important was happening in Catville! Now Catville is a place where lots of important things *do* happen, but this was something almost more important than anything that had ever happened before, and it all had to do with Mr. Count-The-Pennies Tom, the General Manager and President of the Catville Railway Company.

At the very moment the Super Cat alarm clock went off, Mr. Count-The-Pennies Tom opened his eyes, stretched his furry paws and yawned widely. He knew that *this* was the day when he must think very hard indeed about this Very Important Matter. He thought about it all the time he was washing and brushing and dressing himself in front of his big round mirror, and he thought about it when he was putting his red and white striped pyjamas in his bright yellow pyjama case

which had *Mr. Count-The-Pennies Tom* embroidered on the flap. He thought about it as he did his exercises in front of the open window and looked out at the sun which had just risen, and he thought about it while he was lapping his morning milk brought in by Mr. Waiter Tom. He then decided he would go for a brisk walk before breakfast and do some more thinking, for the Very Important Matter must be settled that very day. In any case, fresh air always helped him to think more clearly.

As a matter of fact, Mr. Count-The-Pennies Tom didn't much like thinking of Very Important things before breakfast, but this was something Very Important indeed. It had to do with a train, and as Mr. Count-The-Pennies Tom was very fond of this train he put down his Indian clubs, got his hat and hurried outside into the quiet streets of Catville. Soon he was striding along deep in thought.

Mr. Count-The-Pennies Tom was a big stout cat with tiger stripes. He was wearing a neat black coat and trousers to match, a dazzling white shirt and black silk tie with the letters *C.R.* embroidered in gold all over it. He also wore a pair of daffodil-yellow gloves on his furry paws, and the hat perched on his furry head was the oldest hat in Catville. This hat, which looked for all the world like the tall chimney of a very old steam engine, was called a stove-pipe hat, and although it was now rather battered, it was the very same hat that his Great, Great, Great Grandfather had worn when, years and years ago, *he* had been the first General Manager and President of The Catville Railway Company!

At half-past seven, the church clock in The Square boomed out the half-hour; ding-dong, ding-dong. A minute later, the Town Hall clock boomed out the half-hour too; ding-dong, ding-dong. Mr. Count-The-Pennies Tom glanced at the gold watch which was strapped to his furry wrist to see which clock had boomed out the right time. He could easily tell this because *his* watch was *always* right. As he often said to Mr. Station-Master Tom, "You can't run a railway properly unless you run it to time, and to do this, all your watches and clocks must tell the same time!" A quick peep at his wrist watch was enough to tell him that the church clock was exactly right and that the Town Hall clock was exactly one minute slow.

As Mr. Count-The-Pennies Tom went by, many of the shop-keeping cats and the hurry-off-to-work cats wondered why his handsome eyebrow whiskers were pulled down in such a frown. Usually his furry face was very jolly and bright.

One of the shop-keeping cats who happened to be standing on the pavement when Mr. Count-The-Pennies Tom strolled along, was Mr. Grocer Tom. He had come into the sunny street to pull down the orange and white striped sun-blind outside his shop. Who also should be trotting along the street on his way to the Grammar School but his old friend, Mr. School-Master Tom.

"A lovely morning," said Mr. Grocer Tom, cheerfully.

"It is indeed," said Mr. School-Master Tom, "but Mr. Count-The-Pennies Tom doesn't look very happy this morning, does he? Did you see the frown on his furry face?"

"Yes, I did," said his friend. "I haven't seen him look so gloomy since he closed the Dogville branch line last year."

"That's just it!" cried Mr. School-Master Tom, "he always looks gloomy when he's going to close a branch line."

"You surely don't think he's going to close *another* branch line?" gasped Mr. Grocer Tom.

"If that frown is anything to go by—and I

think it is—then you can be quite sure that he'll be closing another branch line before long," said Mr. School-Master Tom.

"Oh, I *do* hope not," said Mr. Grocer Tom. "I've always loved trains. Train-spotting was my hobby when I was a kitten—still is!"

"I'm a train-spotter, too," said Mr. School-Master Tom. "Do you remember *The Whizzing Wonder* and *The Thursday Thunderer* and *The Snorting Snapdragon?*"

"Yes, I do," said Mr. Grocer Tom, using, to pull down the orange and white striped sun-blind, a long pole with a hook on the end of it. "I also remember *The Catville Conqueror*. Goodness me, that *was* an engine! It was bright scarlet, with a black funnel and lots of shining brass work. I knew the driver, Mr. Full-Speed Ahead Tom. His whiskers are quite grey now, but they were as black as soot in those days."

"I remember once being snowed-up in a train," said Mr. School-Master Tom. "I was coming home from boarding school for Christmas, and luckily we all had food baskets with us. It was very exciting because a gang of hefty working cats had to dig us out with spades before we were taken home on sleighs. What fun it was! Oh, well, I do hope Mr. Count-The-Pennies Tom *won't* close any more branch lines. By the way, we're going on *The Bucket and Spade Express* next week for a day by the sea. Would you like to come?"

"Thank you very much indeed," said his friend, "I'd love to."

Mr. Count-The-Pennies Tom was walking on, still thinking and thinking. He just could not make up his mind. He knew his Great, Great, Great Grandfather would have been horrified at the very idea of *The Picnic Special* ever being taken off, and he, himself, had loved the old train dearly ever since, as a kitten in his mother's arms, he had first travelled up the line to see the wild flowers.

But alas, cats and kittens no longer seemed to love the trains as they once did; they all seemed to prefer cars and buses, scooters and bikes, helicopters and jets . . .

Oh dear! Oh dear! His furry head was beginning to ache with all this thinking!

The church clock now boomed out eight o'clock. Kittens, on their way to the Catville Grammar School in School Lane, ran helter-skelter to the bus stop to catch the special school bus. Their book-filled satchels bobbed on their furry shoulders.

But Mr. Count-The-Pennies Tom did not notice them for he was still thinking very, *very* hard. Suddenly he began to feel very hungry indeed, so he made up his mind to go back to The Station Hotel for his breakfast.

Taking a short cut through the park, he came out by The Catville Opera House—where only last night he had heard a comic opera, by an Italian composing cat named Signor Pussini, called "The Barber Of Catville". Then as he turned down Cobble-Stone Lane, he went into the paper shop and bought a copy of *The Catville News* from Mr. All Sort Tom, the newsagent cat, before continuing towards the hotel.

The Station Hotel stood at the other end of Cobble-Stone Lane. It was a big square stone building with lots and lots of brightly polished windows which were kept clean by

Mr. Window-Cleaning Tom, and lots and lots of rooms which were kept neat and tidy by Miss Spick and Span, the house-keeping cat, and her assistant, Miss Dust and Sweep, the chamber-maid cat. The main entrance or WAY IN, was, of course, at the front, but for travelling cats who came off the trains in the big station which was just behind the hotel, there was another entrance or WAY IN at the back of the station itself. Over the front door was the name of the hotel—THE STATION HOTEL—in big gold letters. Underneath, in smaller letters, was written: "All travelling cats are welcome. Comfortable beds, fur-dressing salon and claw-sharpening parlour. Extra special Fish and Milk menus prepared by our French Chef, Monsieur Le Chat. Kittens catered for. Moderate charges."

Mr. Count-The-Pennies Tom took off his stove-pipe hat with his left paw, pushed the big revolving door with his right paw and walked into the hotel.

"Good morning, sir," said Heave-O, the burly hall porter cat, resplendent in his bright gold uniform.

"Good morning, Heave-O," said Mr. Count-The-Pennies Tom, "I think I'll have my breakfast upstairs this morning instead of going to the dining room, so will you please ask Mr. Waiter Tom to bring up a boiled haddock with a poached egg on top, and a saucer of milk. Haddock always helps me to think better."

"Yes, sir," said Heave-O, "I'll tell him straight away."

Mr. Count-The-Pennies Tom (who was still thinking furiously) trotted across the hall and stepped briskly into the lift. The lift-kitten pressed a button and they were whisked up to the third floor where Mr. Count-The-Pennies Tom stepped briskly out and trotted along the plum-coloured carpeted corridor to room number 107. A few moments later he was sitting in his favourite plum-coloured arm-chair reading his paper. Mr. Count-The-Pennies Tom lived in The Station Hotel so that he could be near his office in the station.

Soon there was a knock on the door. "Come in," called Mr. Count-The-Pennies Tom, putting down his paper. In two twitches

*Mr. Count-The-Pennies Tom sniffed the delicious smell of fresh haddock.*

of a cat's whisker, Mr. Waiter Tom appeared with a tray.

"What do *you* think about *The Picnic Special*?" asked Mr. Count-The-Pennies Tom, as he sniffed the delicious smell of fresh haddock.

"My very favourite train, sir," beamed Mr. Waiter Tom. "We always use it when we want to have a really jolly outing. The kittens love the flowers, the fields and the woods and *we* think it is the finest line in Catville—or anywhere, sir."

"And so do I," said Mr. Count-The-Pennies Tom. "Then you wouldn't want *The Picnic Special* to stop running?"

"Stop running? Oh, my fur and whiskers, I should hope not!" cried Mr. Waiter Tom, looking very upset. "We all love *The Picnic Special*! Please, please, don't take it off, sir."

"Thank you," said Mr. Count-The-Pennies Tom, "I'll have to think very, very carefully indeed about this."

As Mr. Waiter Tom trotted out of the room Mr. Count-The-Pennies Tom began to eat his breakfast. First he ate the poached egg and boiled haddock (leaving the bones, of course!), then he started to lap up the saucer of milk, not stopping until he had lapped up every drop and licked the saucer quite clean with his little pink tongue. Now he sat thinking about how times had changed from the days when he was a tiny kitten who had never, never dreamt that he would one day be General Manager and President of The Catville Railway Company.

Every summer, with his family and friends, he had helped to pack the big picnic hamper with sardine sandwiches, haddock pasties, kipper pies, delicious salmon savouries and large bottles of creamy milk. They had set off for the station in high spirits, wearing sailor hats and sun-bonnets on their furry heads, and thinking of all the fun they would have travelling into the countryside on *The Picnic Special*. His Great, Great, Great Grandfather, his Great, Great Grandfather, his Great Grandfather and his Grandfather, had all travelled on the dear old *Special*. Now he felt very sad indeed at the thought of its never running again, but it simply didn't bring in enough shining copper pennies to pay for keeping it puffing and chuffing up and down between Catville and Marmalade Manor.

How he wished and wished that some bright idea for keeping it going would pop into his furry head. In fact he even wished that he could rub *The Picnic Special* like Aladdin rubbed his lamp, and bring a genie who would turn it into a busy bustling cram-jam-full happy-holiday train again!

## 2　Central Station, Catville

Mr. Count-The-Pennies Tom now got up and went out of his room. He trotted briskly along the plum-coloured carpeted corridor, down the plum-coloured carpeted stairs and along a narrow passage. As he trotted through the door that led into the station, he met Felix, the page-kitten, who was wearing a blue jacket with shining brass buttons down the front.

Felix was carrying a silver salver in his paw and on the silver salver lay a letter, written in green ink and addressed to "Count-The-Pennies Tom, Esq., The General Manager and President of the Catville Railway Company, Central Station, Catville."

"Here is a letter for you, sir," said Felix, holding the silver salver out in front of him.

"Thank you, Felix," said Mr. Count-The-Pennies Tom, taking the letter, "I'll read it in my office."

Popping the letter into his pocket, Mr. Count-The-Pennies Tom trotted up to a door marked: "STRICTLY PRIVATE. This is the Office of Mr. Count-The-Pennies Tom, the General Manager and President of The Catville Railway Company. No CAT MAY COME IN UNLESS ON VERY IMPORTANT BUSINESS INDEED." He pushed open the door and climbed up the steep and wobbly wooden staircase. At the top he pushed open another door and trotted into his long office where a high wooden desk stood beside a big shining window.

Mr. Count-The-Pennies Tom placed his stove-pipe hat on a small table in a corner of the long office. He then sat down at his high wooden desk and looked through the window which was so big that he could see every single thing that was happening in the busy station below. Straight in front of him stood the booking office, which was looked after by Mr. Booking Clerk Tom—the quickest adding-

26

up cat in Catville—and his assistant, Mr. Two and Two (who was often called *Mr. Four*, for short)—the next quickest adding-up cat in Catville. There were two little windows in the booking office. Over one was written FIRST CLASS in big white letters, and over the other was written SECOND CLASS in big yellow letters. On the front of the booking office the letters *C.R.* were painted in gold. They meant, of course, Catville Railways. Indeed the letters *C.R.* were stamped on the red, green and biscuit-coloured tickets, the cups and saucers in the Refreshment Room, the plates and spoons and curtains in the Station Hotel, the tablecloths and electric light bulbs in the dining cars and the sides of the engines and coaches—every single thing in fact that belonged to the Catville Railway Company.

Standing at Platform 10 was Mr. Count-The-Pennies Tom's very own private coach. He travelled in this whenever he wanted to go and visit the other stations on the Catville Railway, and this was quite often. This coach was like a sitting room on wheels. It had arm-chairs and reading lamps and was called a

SALOON. On either side were stamped not only the letters *C.R.* but a picture of Mr. Count-The-Pennies Tom's own furry head as well!

Near the booking office stood the bright green bookstall where travelling gentlemen cats could buy *The Catville News* and *The Catville Times*, travelling lady cats could buy *Lady Cat's Own* and travelling kittens, *Playful Kittens*. Beside the bookstall stood the Refreshment Room, which was looked after by Miss Tasty Paws. There the travelling cats and kittens could get all kinds of delicious snacks and, of course, saucers of milk. To the right of the Refreshment Room stood the Left Luggage Office.

Meanwhile, Mr. Waiter Tom had told many of the other cats how Mr. Count-The-Pennies Tom had asked him about *The Picnic Special*.

"*Non! Non!*" cried Monsieur Le Chat, the French Chef. He was a huge cream-coloured cat with deep copper eyes. A tall snow-white hat was perched on his furry head.

"Stop running *The Picnic Special*!" cried

28

the Hotel Manager, Mr. Rush-About Tom. "What a dreadful idea! Why, *my* kittens would be heart-broken!"

"And mine!" cried Heave-O. "Why, my Great Granny used to tell us tales of the grand picnics *she* had at Marmalade Manor."

"I remember the time *The Picnic Special* had one of her breakdowns," said Mr. Waiter Tom. "We all had to eat our food in the carriages and they gave us our fares back when we got home."

Back at the station, Mr. Engine-Driver Tom was bringing in *The Flying Scotscat*. With a hiss of steam and a grinding of brakes it stopped exactly six inches from the shining buffers beside Platform 2. Amongst the travelling cats who descended was Mr. MacPherson Tom, a handsome cat with snow-white shirt and paws to match. He sold Edinburgh Rock and tartan umbrellas in the shop in Piper's Way. A porter cat heaved Mr. MacPherson Tom's luggage on to a truck and followed him down the platform to where a little blue motor car was waiting. Mr. MacPherson Tom had been to Scotland and under his furry arm he carried his bagpipes and a box of Edinburgh Rock. Looking out of his big glass window, Mr. Count-The-Pennies Tom watched Mr. Mac-Pherson Tom striding along towards Mr. Mackintosh, the wild cat, who played the bagpipes in the Catville Town Band. Mr. Mackintosh had come to meet his friend.

"I wish the poor old *Picnic Special* was as full as *these* trains," thought Mr. Count-The-Pennies Tom.

Platform 4 was very busy. There, a train with twelve coaches and a big red engine was waiting to take cat families to the seaside. A lady announcing-cat suddenly spoke over the station loud-speaker: "The train now standing at Platform 4 is *The Bucket and Spade Express.* It will arrive in Catmint-on-Sea in two hours and two minutes." Soon after that, the guard blew his whistle and waved his green flag, and with a hoot and a toot, the long train began to move out of the station. It was packed tight with happy holiday-making cats and kittens, all on their way to the seaside, and Mr. Count-The-Pennies Tom knew that the train wouldn't stop until it arrived in Catmint-on-Sea—exactly on time.

Standing at Platform 5 were chocolate and cream coloured coaches and the green diesel-electric engine of *The Catville Flyer*. This

left Catville every morning at ten o'clock, winter and summer alike. It went to Cat Hills, an old country town in the County of Catshire, which was surrounded by a big stone wall built by Roman cats years and years ago!

All the express trains that ran on the main lines, and nearly all the stopping trains that ran on the branch lines, had brightly painted engines and coaches. They were hardly ever late. However, there was one train that *never* ran to time, and that was the poor old *Picnic Special*. It had battered old coaches with dirty windows and torn seats, and a little tiger of a tank engine called *Puffing Pussy*. Its chimney was as rusty as an old tin can.

The *Picnic Special* ran every day in summer and winter whether wet or fine. It wound its way through the prettiest scenery in Catshire, and, once upon a time, when it was a brand-new train and *Puffing Pussy* looked shining and bright in her red and gold paint, dozens and dozens of picnicking cats and kittens loved to go on it for a day out in the country. Nowadays, alas, its coaches were so grubby and *Puffing Pussy* broke down so often (because she needed a new boiler and some oil on her wheels) that fewer and fewer cats and kittens wanted to travel on it. Strange as it may seem, no one—not even Mr. Count-The-Pennies Tom himself—really knew why

*The Picnic Special* had not been kept spick and span like all the other trains.

Once more, the lady announcing-cat began to speak over the station loud-speaker: "The train now standing at Platform I is *The Picnic Special*, which leaves Catville for Marmalade Manor every morning as the fingers of the station clock point to half-past nine. It will call at Whisker Junction, Marmalade Mansion Halt, Thistle Junction, Marmalade Farm, Buttercup Halt, Daisy Meadow, Dandelion Point, Daffodil Corner (Low Level), and Marmalade Manor (for Marigold Lane)."

Mr. Count-The-Pennies Tom looked through his big window to see how many cats and kittens were going to travel on *The Picnic Special*. There were so few that he could easily count them on the claws of his right paw! "Miaow!" he said to himself. "I've made up my mind at last about that Very Important Matter!" And then and there, he took a sheet of clean white paper and wrote out two big notices. When he had finished, he gave them to a page-kitten and told him to take one to *The Catville News* and the other to *The Catville Times*.

As the page-kitten trotted out of the office, Mr. Count-The-Pennies Tom suddenly remembered the letter that he had popped in his pocket. He drew it out, and looked at the writing on the envelope. In small, neat writing it read: "Count-The-Pennies Tom, Esq., The General Manager and President of The Catville Railway Company, Central Station, Catville." The "Esq." was, of course, short for "Esquire". Mr. Count-The-Pennies Tom opened the envelope with a silver letter-opener, and spreading out the letter on the desk in front of him, he popped his spectacles on his furry nose and began to read.

22 Furry Avenue,
Catville.

Telephone Number: CAT 25.

Dear Mr. Count-The-Pennies Tom,
    I teach a class of thirty kittens in the Sunday School, and should like to take them for a picnic on Tuesday, July, the 20th, to

Marigold Lane. Will you please keep thirty seats for the kittens and one seat for myself on *The Picnic Special*.

>     With many purrs,
>         Yours sincerely,
>             Shani, the Siamese.

"Too late!" cried Mr. Count-The-Pennies Tom, and he lifted the telephone receiver and dialled CAT 25 with his furry paw. . . .

## 3  *The News is announced*

Early the next morning, the sprightly young paper-kitten, Tiger Tompkins, and his young brother Titus, who helped him to deliver the papers, arrived at Mr. All Sort Tom's shop in Cobble-Stone Lane. Mr. All Sort Tom said, "There's some very important news in the papers this morning, so do be quite sure that all the newspaper-reading cats get their papers." Tiger Tompkins and Titus promised that they would, and when they had popped the papers through the letter-boxes of all the newspaper-reading cats, they jumped on their bicycles and rode off to school.

A little later, in the Marmalade Milk Bar, Mr. Marmalade was standing behind the counter. A snow-white apron was tied round his furry middle, and he was busily polishing some clean saucers with a snow-white polishing cloth. When all the saucers were polished, he stacked them one on top of another, until there was a little round tower of saucers standing on the counter.

While he was waiting for his first customer, Mr. Marmalade made up his mind to read *The Catville News* which was lying folded up on the counter beside the tower of saucers. When he spread the paper out in front of him, he was very surprised indeed, for there, in the middle of the front page, was a notice printed in big black letters. This is what it said:

### A NOTICE ABOUT
### A VERY IMPORTANT MATTER

"Mr. Count-The-Pennies Tom, the President and General Manager of The Catville Railway Company, has made up his mind to CLOSE the branch line and stop running *The Picnic Special*. For a long, long time, hardly any cats or kittens have travelled on this train, and, because of this, *The Picnic Special* doesn't earn enough pennies to pay the engine-driver cat and the guard their wages. Mr. Count-The-Pennies Tom is sorry to say that when this line is closed (which will be SOON), the following stations will be closed to travelling cats and kittens: Whisker Junction, Marmalade Mansion Halt, Thistle Junction, Marmalade Farm, Buttercup Halt, Daisy Meadow, Dandelion Point, Daffodil Corner (Low Level), and Marmalade Manor. But Mr. Count-The-Pennies Tom also wishes to say that these stations will stay open for the goods trains that bring coal, tins of sardines, fresh fish, and, of course, bottles of rich creamy milk from Mr. Marmalade's Farm."

When he had read every word in the notice, Mr. Marmalade put the paper down, and, rubbing his furry chin with his paw, began to think. . . .

Meanwhile, in the big shop with the little window on the other side of the street, sat Mr Marmalade's friend, Mr. Black Tom, who sold the most delicious fish in Catville. He was sitting at his desk, his spectacles on his furry nose, reading exactly the same notice on the front page of *The Catville Times*. When he had read every word, *he* was very surprised, too.

"Smoky," said Mr. Black Tom to his errand-kitten, who was weighing some fresh cod on the big brass scales, "come here a moment and read this." Smoky wiped his paws on a clean blue and white striped cloth, then began to read the notice in the paper. When he had read every word, Mr. Black Tom asked him what he thought about it.

"I think it's a shame!" cried Smoky.

"And I think it's a shame, too," said Mr. Black Tom.

"When I was a tiny kitten, I often went on *The Picnic Special* for a day out in the country," said Smoky.

"So did I," said Mr. Black Tom, standing up, "and now I'll just go over the road and see what Mr. Marmalade thinks about it."

Leaving Smoky in charge of the fish shop, Mr. Black Tom folded the paper and put it in his pocket, popped his best straw hat on his furry head and hurried out of the shop. Looking first to the right, then to the left, and then to the right again, he made quite sure that there were no big red motor buses, rumbling lorries or cars coming before he trotted briskly over the road. He didn't stop until he was sitting on a high stool at the counter of the milk bar.

"Good morning, Mr. Marmalade," said Mr. Black Tom.

"Good morning, Mr. Black Tom," said Mr. Marmalade, politely, "and what brings you out so early in the morning?"

"This!" cried Mr. Black Tom, bringing *The Catville Times* out of his pocket with a flourish. "What do you think of that?"

"Peru!" said Mr. Marmalade, "I've already seen it in *The Catville News* and I think it's a shame!"

"That's just what Smoky and I said when we read it," agreed his friend.

"Peru!" said Mr. Marmalade, pushing a saucer of rich creamy milk carefully across the counter to Mr. Black Tom. "Have a saucer of milk and then we'll put our furry heads together and try to think of some way to keep *The Picnic Special* running."

After Mr. Black Tom had lapped up every drop of milk, he said, "I can always think better after I've had some of your rich creamy milk."

*"Smoky . . . come here a moment and read this."*

41

That afternoon the sun was shining brightly in a sky that was as blue as Mrs. Tabby's brand-new cushion covers. Mr. Ali Baba, the Proud Persian, who kept the curio shop in The Square, had made up his mind to go for his walk earlier than usual. The weather-forecasting cat on the wireless had said that there might be a shower of rain later in the day, and there was nothing Mr. Ali Baba disliked more than getting wet. So, popping on his straw hat and picking up his silver-handled cane, he trotted out of the curio shop and strolled leisurely round the streets of Catville, looking into the shop windows. At the corner of Felix Road, he met Mr. Weatherwise Tom, who was something of a weather prophet. Mr. Ali Baba told him what the weather-forecasting cat had said, but Mr. Weatherwise Tom only burst out laughing and said, "Don't you believe it! Weather-forecasting cats are sometimes *wrong*! I can tell you that it won't rain to-day."

"But how do you know it won't rain?" asked Mr. Ali Baba.

"Because my whiskers always twitch when it's going to rain, and they are not twitching the least little bit at the moment, are they?" said Mr. Weatherwise Tom. Mr. Ali Baba had to agree that they weren't!

On his way back to The Square, Mr. Ali Baba met Mr. Marmalade's friend, Miss Tilly Tortoiseshell, who sold mittens in her little shop with the round window. She was coming out of Fish Alley—a short cut leading to Marmalade Avenue. This was named after Mr. Marmalade's uncle, Squire Marmalade, who had gone to America to make his fortune.

"Good afternoon, Miss Tilly Tortoiseshell," said Mr. Ali Baba, sweeping off his straw hat and bowing very low, "it is a lovely day, isn't it?"

"It is, indeed," agreed Miss Tilly Tortoiseshell, who was wearing a blue and white spotted frock with a big white cartwheel hat on her furry head and carrying a small bag, "and that is *one* reason why I came out for a walk," she added.

"And what was the other reason?" asked Mr. Ali Baba, politely.

"To *think*," replied Miss Tilly Tortoiseshell, promptly. "You see, I always think better when I'm out walking in the fresh air."

"And what are you thinking about?" Mr. Ali Baba asked.

"About a Very Important Matter," she said.

"Is it the same Very Important Matter that was in the paper this morning?" Mr. Ali Baba wanted to know.

"The very same!" cried Miss Tilly Tortoiseshell.

"And *I'm* thinking about it, too," said Mr. Ali Baba.

"Then perhaps *you* can help me?" she said, and Mr. Ali Baba replied that he would be delighted to help her if he could.

"Well," said Miss Tilly Tortoiseshell, "my friend, Miss Shani, the Siamese, who has come to live at Number 22 Furry Avenue, is very upset indeed. You see, she came a long, long way from Foreign Parts to live in Catville and ever since she came to the town, she's been teaching a class of thirty kittens in the Sunday School."

Mr. Ali Baba nodded his furry head, and said that he had met Miss Shani only the other week when she had come into his shop to buy a curio.

"Well, last week," Miss Tilly Tortoiseshell went on, "Miss Shani promised to take her class of kittens on *The Picnic Special* for a day out in the country, but when she wrote to Mr. Count-The-Pennies Tom about it, he rang her up straight away to say that he was going to close the line. The kittens *will* be disappointed."

"And how do you want me to help you?" asked Mr. Ali Baba.

"Can *you* think of a bright idea that would make Mr. Count-The-Pennies Tom change his mind and keep the branch line open?" she asked.

Mr. Ali Baba rubbed his furry chin and began to think, but after he had thought for a moment he shook his head and said, "*I* can't think of anything, but why not go and ask Mr. Marmalade? He's *sure* to think of a bright idea!"

"Thank you, Mr. Ali Baba," said Miss Tilly

Tortoiseshell, "I'll go and see him now and I'll take Miss Shani with me."

"And I'll come, too!" cried Mr. Ali Baba.

They took the first turning on the right, the second on the left and third on the right again, until they came to Furry Avenue. Just as they were about to walk up the steps of Number 22, the front door opened wide, and Miss Shani herself appeared and walked sedately down the steps. She looked very cool in a green and white spotted frock with a big white cartwheel hat on her head.

Mr. Ali Baba swept off his straw hat and bowed deeply. "Miss Shani, the Siamese," he said, "I have never seen a cat with such lovely blue eyes before! Why, they're as blue as the deep blue sea at Fish Bay!"

"Thank you, Mr. Ali Baba," said Miss Shani, speaking in a most unusual voice, which was not a bit like any other voice in Catville, except perhaps Mr. Min-Pye-Toy's voice (the travelling beauty-specialist cat). This wasn't the least bit surprising as he was a Siamese and came from Foreign Parts, too! "You see," she went on, "we Siamese are very unusual, indeed!"

"I'm sure you are," murmured Mr. Ali Baba, politely.

"Yes," Miss Shani continued, "and *I* do some very odd things, too!"

"Do you?" murmured Mr. Ali Baba.

"Yes. One odd thing I do is to have a bath in water nine times a day," said Miss Shani. "Of course, I don't bathe myself, oh, dear me, no! I get my maid-kitten, Annette—she's French, you know—to hold her paw under the tap and rub my coat all over with water.

When I've had enough I give her a gentle bite to let her know that she can stop. I have three baths in the morning, three in the afternoon and three at night. I'm sure not many cats do that!"

"I'm quite sure they don't!" said Mr. Ali Baba, who shuddered at the very idea of being washed in *water*.

"We were just coming to take you to see Mr. Marmalade," said Miss Tilly Tortoise-shell, "for we are hoping that he may be able to think of a bright idea to keep *The Picnic Special* running."

"Oh, I *do* hope so!" cried Miss Shani, clapping her paws, "because I don't want to disappoint my class of Sunday School kittens."

"Come on, then, let's go and see him now," said Miss Tilly Tortoiseshell.

"Here's a taxi!" cried Mr. Ali Baba, who was standing at the edge of the pavement waving his silver-handled cane for the taxi to stop. Mr. Taxi-Driver Tom drove his daffodil-yellow taxi to the kerbside. When they were all seated inside, Mr. Ali Baba told Mr. Taxi-Driver Tom to drive them to the

Marmalade Milk Bar, and in no time at all they were whisked through the streets to their destination. Mr. Ali Baba jumped out first, politely held open the door and helped his friends down. Then he paid Mr. Taxi-Driver Tom one silver shilling, and the taxi drove off.

"The milk bar seems to be closed," said Miss Tilly Tortoiseshell.

"It *is* closed," said Mr. Ali Baba, "but I see there's a notice in the window."

"Let's go and read it," said Miss Shani.

So they trotted up to the window and Miss Tilly Tortoiseshell read the notice aloud.

" 'The Marmalade Milk Bar,' " she read, " ' will be closed this afternoon. If any of Mr. Marmalade's friends wish to see him, will they please go over to the fish shop, where he is holding a Very Important Meeting about a Very Important Matter. All are welcome. A collection of silver sixpences and shillings will be taken, but for those who can't afford to give any silver, there will also be a collection of copper pennies. Mr. Marmalade is holding the meeting in Mr. Black Tom's big sitting room because his own sitting room is too small.' "

"Come on!" cried Mr. Ali Baba, "it looks as though Mr. Marmalade has already thought of a bright idea!"

## 4  *A Very Important Meeting*

At the fish shop they found Smoky dressed in his best Sunday suit, waiting to show all the visiting cats into the big sitting room behind the shop.

"What is the meeting about, Smoky?" asked Mr. Ali Baba.

"I don't know *exactly* what it is about," said Smoky, "but I *do* know it's about a Very Important Matter. Please come into the sitting room and join the others."

Miss Shani and Miss Tilly Tortoiseshell and Mr. Ali Baba, followed Smoky along a dark passage and as they came nearer and nearer to the closed door of the sitting room, the murmur of cat voices grew louder and louder.

Flinging open the door, Smoky shouted at the top of his voice, "Miss Shani, the Siamese,

Miss Tilly Tortoiseshell, and Mr. Ali Baba, the Proud Persian."

The hum and buzz of talk died away and Mr. Black Tom, who was standing beside Mr. Marmalade at the far end of the room, said, "You are just in time, for we are about to begin our Very Important Meeting. Please show them to their seats, Smoky."

Safely settled in her seat, Miss Tilly Tortoiseshell looked round the sitting room. It was packed tight with cats; indeed, she had never seen so many cats crowded together in one room before. Sitting on her right was Miss Inky-Paws, the reporting cat on *The Catville News*. She was ready with her notebook and pencil to take down in writing every word that was going to be said.

Mr. Black Tom clapped his paws together for silence. "Lady cats and gentlemen cats," he said, "Mr. Marmalade and I have asked you to come here this afternoon to talk about a Very Important Matter." There was a pause. "We were all kittens once, weren't we?" he continued, and all the cats nodded their furry heads as he paused again. "Well, then," went on Mr. Black Tom, "I'm sure we must all remember going for picnics on *The Picnic Special.*" He paused once more, and all the cats cried, "Hear! Hear!" and tears began to roll down one or two furry faces as they remembered the happy times they had had on *The Picnic Special.* "Now we've all read in our papers this morning," said Mr. Black Tom, "how Mr. Count-The-Pennies Tom is going to stop *The Picnic Special.* The branch line for travelling cats and kittens to Marmalade Manor is to close because it doesn't make enough money to pay the engine driver cat and the guard their wages!"

"I'm not a wee bit surprised at that," said Mr. MacPherson Tom. "To begin with, the engine, *Puffing Pussy* needs a new boiler, for the one she has now is cracked." (He called *Puffing Pussy* "she" because railway engines, like ships, are always spoken of as if they were ladies).

"And she needs re-painting!" cried his friend, Mr. Mackintosh, the wild cat.

"And she needs oil on her wheels, which are always squeaking!" cried Mr. Ali Baba.

"And the coaches are in a disgraceful state with torn seats and dirty windows," said Miss Tilly Tortoiseshell.

"Peru!" cried Mr. Marmalade, "and *that's* the very reason why hardly any cats or kittens ever travel on it!"

"Somehow," said Mr. Black Tom, "we must try and persuade Mr. Count-The-Pennies Tom to let Miss Shani take her class of thirty kittens on *The Picnic Special* for their outing on July the 20th, even though the coaches *are* in such a disgraceful state."

"I quite agree," said Mr. Ali Baba, "we simply can't disappoint a class of thirty kittens."

"Hear! Hear!" and "Miaow!" cried all the cats.

Then up jumped Mr. Bambi Black. He looked after the Wayside Marmalade Milk Bar which was near to Marmalade Farm, where Mr. Marmalade's cows, Polly, Daisy, Tulip, Buttercup, Cherry and Wenna grazed. "We must do more than that!" he stated. "We must persuade him to keep the line open for good, for, as you all know, some of my customers at the Wayside Milk Bar come by train to Marmalade Farm. Why, I sell lots of rich creamy ice-cream in the summer and lots of warm milk in the winter to thirsty train-travelling cats and kittens. I also serve all the motoring, scootering, cycling, and walking cats, too!"

"Hear! Hear!" and "Miaow!" cried all the cats again.

"Peru!" cried Mr. Marmalade, "I'm afraid that Mr. Count-The-Pennies Tom has quite made up his mind to close the line, but even so, I think that *I* know how the line can be kept open, though it isn't going to be easy."

"You *do*!" cried Mr. Macpherson Tom.

"Yes," said Mr. Marmalade, "I was on the phone to Mr. Count-The-Pennies Tom an hour ago, and I asked him if he would agree to sell *The Picnic Special* and the branch line to Marmalade Manor. He said he would, but he wants so many silver shillings and sixpences and copper pennies that we're going to have a hard job to find them all!"

"How many silver sixpences and silver shillings does he want?" asked Mr. Ali Baba.

"Peru!" cried **Mr.** Marmalade, "he wants one sack filled until it is bulging with silver sixpences and another sack filled until it is bulging with silver shillings!"

"And how many copper pennies does he want, Mr. Marmalade?" asked Mrs. Tabby.

"Peru!" said Mr. Marmalade, "he wants one shining black Wellington boot filled to the brim with copper pennies!"

"That *is* a lot," said Mrs. Tabby, opening her pillar-box red purse, "but I can give you one copper penny to start off with," and she held out a brand-new copper penny.

"Thank you, Mrs. Tabby," said Mr. Marmalade, politely.

"And here's one of my shining black Wellington boots to put it in!" cried Mr. Black Tom. Mrs. Tabby dropped her brand-new copper penny into the shining black Wellington boot.

"I'll give you a silver shilling," said Mr. Mackintosh.

Mr. Baker Tom unfolded a brand-new empty flour sack that he'd brought from his bakehouse. It had a label pinned on it with the words SILVER SHILLINGS printed in big black letters. "Here is the very sack," he said.

As soon as Mr. Mackintosh had dropped his silver shilling into the sack, Mr. MacPherson Tom said that he would give a silver shilling, too.

Then Mr. Baker Tom unfolded another brand-new empty flour sack that he'd brought from his bakehouse, and this one had a label pinned on it with the words SILVER SIXPENCES printed in big blue letters.

"And *I'll* give a silver sixpence," exclaimed Miss Inky-Paws, who was writing down everything that they said in her note book.

When every single cat in Mr. Black Tom's sitting room had given something, Mr. Marmalade thanked them very politely and said that the sack for silver shillings would be kept in the Marmalade Milk Bar. Mr. Black Tom said that the sack for silver sixpences would be kept in the fish shop, and Mr. Ali Baba said that he would take the shining black Wellington boot for copper pennies and place it on the counter of the curio shop.

Soon after that, the meeting broke up, and

Mr. Marmalade's friends promised to tell him straight away if they had any bright ideas about raising money to save the branch line. Mr. Black Tom hung the sack for silver sixpences on a hook in the fish shop, and Mr. Ali Baba proudly bore the shining black Wellington boot through the streets (collecting some copper pennies from passers-by as he did so) and placed it on the counter of his curio shop. Mr. Marmalade hung the sack for silver shillings on a hat-stand in the milk bar.

## 5  *A bright idea*

When Mr. Marmalade and those cats who took *The Catville News* looked at their papers next morning, the front page headline written by Miss Inky-Paws read:

HELP TO SAVE THE MARIGOLD LINE

Underneath, in small black letters, was printed every single word that had been spoken by Mr. Marmalade and his friends at the Very Important Meeting. Again, when those cats who took *The Catville Times* looked at *their* papers, they found on the front page the very same headline and the very same report. Miss Inky-Paws had sent all that she had written about the meeting to *both* papers, the news being so very important.

"Peru!" cried Mr. Marmalade, when Mr. Black Tom came into the milk bar for his mid-morning saucer of milk. "If we are able to save enough money to buy *The Picnic Special* branch line, *we'll* call it *The Marigold Line* and we'll call the train that runs on it *The Marigold Special*. I think that Miss Inky-Paws has thought of a wonderful name!"

"I agree," said his friend, dropping a silver shilling into the sack that was hanging on the hat-stand near the counter.

Mr. Black Tom sat down on a high stool, and after he had lapped up a saucer of milk, he said, "Yes, *The Marigold Line* is a very good name for the branch line, and *The Marigold Special* is a very good name for the train, because, as we all know, the grassy mounds on either side of the single track are crowded every summer with more marigolds than there are cats in Catville!"

While Mr. Marmalade and Mr. Black Tom were talking, Mr. Marmalade's sister, Miss Candy-Stripe (or "Toffee", as he called her, because she had toffee-coloured stripes and white paws), trotted into the shop. She took a silver shilling out of her purse, dropped it into the sack, and then sat down beside Mr. Black Tom.

*The Catville newspapers had reported the meeting in full.*

"Hallo! Mr. Black Tom," said Toffee, nodding her head.

"Hallo!" replied Mr. Black Tom.

"Hallo! Orange," she said to Mr. Marmalade. (She always called him "Orange" because he really was the colour of Marmalade.)

"Here's a saucer of milk for you, dear sister," said Mr. Marmalade, carefully pushing a saucer of rich creamy milk across the counter.

"Thank you, Orange," said Toffee, and while she was slowly lapping up the milk she thought how wonderful it was to be living in Catville.

Toffee had The Kitten Shop in the High Street. She sold clockwork mice, rattles, pretty dolls exactly like Miss Tilly Tortoiseshell and Miss Shani, books with stories and pictures, coats, hats and even prams. Everything, in fact, that kittens needed. The shop was rented from Mr. Builder Tom, and when Toffee had asked him what the rent would be, he had promptly said, "One clockwork mouse every Friday at two o'clock in the afternoon." Mr. Marmalade had been very amused. "Aren't you a bit *old* for clockwork mice," he said. Mr. Builder Tom had replied with twinkling eyes, "Not at all—you see, I'm still very much a kitten at heart!"

Before she came to live in Catville, Toffee had lived at Mouse View, Cat Lane, Cat Hill, Catshire, and she remembered, as she lapped up the last drop of milk, how Mr. Marmalade had been her very first customer in Catville. "Peru!" he had said, "May *I* have a clockwork mouse, please?" Toffee had replied, "What do *you* want with a clockwork mouse, dear brother?" Mr. Marmalade had laughed and said, "Peru! I want to play with it, of course! You see, *I'm* still a kitten at heart, too!"

Mr. Marmalade told Toffee all about how he was going to call the branch line, *The Marigold Line*, and that he had just heard that Mr. Count-The-Pennies Tom was going to stop running *The Picnic Special* or *The Marigold Special*, as it was to be called, on July the 10th.

"That is exactly one whole month from now, for to-day is June the 10th," said Toffee.

"That's right," said Mr. Marmalade, "so you see, we have just one whole month in which to get sufficient silver sixpences and shillings and copper pennies to buy the railway."

"It isn't very long," said Mr. Black Tom, gloomily.

"It's long enough to work wonders, if we try very hard!" cried a lilting voice from the doorway. "My name," it continued, "is Mr. Daffadowndilly Tom and I'm a Welsh cat from Brecon Beacons. I'm full of bright ideas, I talk a lot and, what's more, I'm a champion singing cat!"

"Peru!" cried Mr. Marmalade, very impressed. "Come and have some milk."

"Thank you," said the Welsh cat. He dropped a silver shilling into the sack, and then with a leap and a bound, he sat down on a stool beside Toffee and Mr. Black Tom.

After he had lapped up every drop of milk, Mr. Daffadowndilly Tom told them that for generations, his family had been station cats in Wales, London and Glasgow. "I was a station cat in the Isle of Man myself until I retired," he concluded, "so you see we are a *family* of station cats."

"And what exactly was your job when you were a station cat?" asked Mr. Black Tom. "I'm sure it was very important."

"Indeed, yes!" said the Welsh cat. "My job was to keep the mice out of the Refreshment Rooms!"

"Which I am quite sure you did very well," said Mr. Black Tom.

"I certainly *did*," said Mr. Daffadowndilly Tom.

"Now then," said Mr. Marmalade, "can anyone think of a bright idea to raise all the money that we'll need to pay Mr. Count-The-Pennies Tom for *The Marigold Line*?"

"Indeed, I can think of one idea," said the Welsh cat. "I'll hire the Catville Opera House and give a concert of popular cat songs. All the money I make I will give to you, Mr. Marmalade, for *The Marigold Line*."

"Peru!" said Mr. Marmalade, rubbing his paws, "Now that is a good idea."

At that very moment, the door opened again, and Mr. MacPherson Tom and his friend, Mr. Mackintosh, the wild cat, came in. They told Mr. Marmalade that *they* would arrange a Scottish evening and have a Special Fish Haggis Supper for all the cats.

"*Fish* haggis!" cried Mr. Black Tom. "I've never heard of that before."

"Neither have I!" said Toffee.

"Och aye!" said Mr. MacPherson Tom. "You've never heard of it because it simply didn't exist until I invented it this morning!"

"Perhaps *we* could hire the Catville Opera House too," said Mr. Mackintosh. "After we've had our programme of dances and bagpipe tunes, we could serve our Special Fish Haggis Supper on the stage!"

"A good idea, that is," said the Welsh cat. "Come with me and we'll go and see the manager cat of the Opera House."

After they had said "good day" to Mr. Marmalade and his friends, Mr. Mackintosh, Mr. MacPherson Tom and Mr. Daffadowndilly Tom, trotted out of the milk bar and boarded a Number 9 bus to the Catville Opera House. There they met Mr. Bow and Smile Tom, the manager cat. He listened to their plan and then said they could have the Opera House next Tuesday night.

"And how much will it cost us to hire the Opera House?" asked the Welsh cat.

"Nothing! Nothing at all!" cried Mr. Bow and Smile Tom. "You see, *I* want to save *The Marigold Line*, too! And what is more," he went on, "I will fix up some trestle tables on the stage as soon as you have finished your musical evening. Your Special Fish Haggis Supper can be cooked in the Opera House kitchen and, when it is ready, the ice-cream and chocolate selling cats will help you to serve it."

The Welsh cat and his Scottish friends were just delighted and they thanked Mr. Bow and Smile Tom very politely indeed.

Outside the stage door of the Opera House, they met their old friend, Mr. Printer Tom. He was extremely interested when *he* heard that they were holding a concert and Special Fish Haggis Supper, and he promised to print some brightly-coloured posters. "As soon as they're printed," said Mr. Printer Tom, "I'll stick one up on every single notice board in Catville. All the cats and kittens will then know about your concert and supper!

Now I'll go straight back to my printing shop and start work."

That night Mr. Printer Tom stayed up very late indeed printing the posters. Early next morning, he stacked them into his little yellow motor van and drove off to the first notice board. Once the first poster was up, he drove off to the next notice board, and in no time at all he had stuck a big poster on every single notice board in Catville, just as he had said he would.

"What a splendid poster!" cried Mr. Jolly Jumbo Tom, the jumbo-size cat who was the biggest cat in the world.

"Please read it aloud to me. I am short-sighted—just can't see much farther than the end of my whiskers—and I've left my spectacles at home," said Mr. Bat and Ball, the owner of the Sports Shop in Kippered Herring Lane. He sold cricket bats and balls, wickets, and knee-pads, hockey sticks, footballs, tennis rackets and tennis balls, swimsuits, white canvas shoes with stout rubber soles, white shirts for cross-country running and paper-chasing cats, ping-pong tables, bats and balls—indeed, he sold every possible thing that the sporting cat could possibly need.

"Certainly! I'll read it," said Mr. Jolly Jumbo Tom, twitching his long white whiskers. "Here goes!"

"'MR. DAFFADOWNDILLY TOM, the FAMOUS Welsh Singing Cat, and his friends, Mr. MacPherson Tom and Mr. Mackintosh, the FAMOUS Scottish Piping and Dancing Cats, are giving a GRAND CONCERT followed by a SPECIAL FISH HAGGIS SUPPER on the stage of The Catville Opera House on Tuesday next at 7 p.m. All ticket money that they make at this concert will be given to Mr. Marmalade to HELP TO BUY THE MARIGOLD LINE. Tickets are One Silver Shilling for the VERY, VERY BEST SEATS, One Silver Sixpence for the VERY BEST SEATS, and One Copper Penny for the BEST SEATS.'"

When Mr. Jolly Jumbo Tom had read the notice, Mr. Bat and Ball said, "I'm quite sure that every single ticket will soon be sold."

And of course he was right! All the tickets *were* sold and on Tuesday night the Opera

House was packed full with excited cats and kittens. Mr. Daffadowndilly Tom sang his songs, Mr. MacPherson Tom danced the Highland Fling, and Mr. Mackintosh played his bagpipes. The cats and kittens in the audience clapped their furry paws. They then trotted up on the big stage and sat down at the long trestle tables that Mr. Bow and Smile Tom had quickly fixed up as soon as the concert had ended. The Special Fish Haggis Supper was cooked to a turn by Mr. Mac-Pherson Tom and Mr. Mackintosh and it was served by the ice-cream and chocolate-selling cats. Everyone thoroughly enjoyed themselves.

At the end of the evening, Mr. Bow and Smile Tom went into his office at the front of the Opera House. There he began to count all the shillings, sixpences and pennies that the cats and kittens had paid for their tickets. There were a great many silver coins, but not nearly enough to fill the sack for silver shillings in the milk bar or the sack for silver sixpences in the fish shop. There *were*, however, just enough pennies to fill the shining black Wellington boot to the brim.

Next day, Mr. Ali Baba proudly carried the shining black Wellington boot filled with copper pennies to the milk bar. Mr. Marmalade was very pleased indeed. "Peru!" he

purred, "we have all the copper pennies we need. Now we must try very hard to think of a way to fill the silver shilling and sixpenny sacks."

"I quite agree," said his friend, Mr. Black Tom. "Let's put our furry heads together and try to think of another bright idea to raise some more money."

"That's a good idea," said Mr. Marmalade.

"*I'm* going to see Mr. Smile Please Tom, later to-day," said Mr. Ali Baba. "I'll ask him if *he* has any bright ideas to raise money for *The Marigold Line*."

## 6 "Happy Snaps"

Mr. Smile Please Tom, the jolly photographer cat, sold brand-new cameras in the little shop with the green tiled roof that stood at the corner of Paw Alley and Whisker Lane. He also sold rolls of film for taking black and white and colour photographs and big albums in which his cat customers could stick their snapshots. When cats and kittens came to his shop to have their photographs taken, he led them through a green baize door at the back of the shop into a little room lit by very bright lights. This he called his *studio*.

About the time that Mr. Marmalade and his friends were putting their furry heads together, Mrs. Tabby was taking her youngest kitten, Matilda, to have her photograph taken. Matilda was wearing her best party frock, and had a pretty pink bow tied on the tip of her furry tail. In her arms she held one of the new "Mr. Marmalade" dolls (made, of course, by Mr. Jolly Jumbo Tom, the toy-making cat), which looked exactly like Mr. Marmalade when he was a kitten.

Mr. Smile Please Tom developed the colour photograph later that afternoon and he was so delighted with it that he made up his mind to show it at once to Mr. Marmalade. He carefully slipped it into an envelope, then fixed a "CLOSED. GONE TO SEE MR. MARMALADE. OPEN WHEN I COME BACK AGAIN." notice in the window as he left the shop. Off he trotted briskly down Whisker Lane, not stopping until he was sitting on a high stool at the counter of the milk bar.

"Hallo! Mr. Marmalade," cried Mr. Smile Please Tom, placing the envelope on the counter. "I'm very excited to-day and when I'm very excited I get very thirsty."

"Peru!" cried Mr. Marmalade, pushing a saucer of milk across the counter, "then what you need is some milk! There's nothing like rich creamy milk for thirsty cats, and this milk is the richest and creamiest in all Catville, for it comes from Wenna, my Welsh

74

Black cow!" When Mr. Smile Please Tom had lapped up every drop and licked the saucer quite clean, Mr. Marmalade said, "Peru! And what are you excited about?"

"This!" cried Mr. Smile Please Tom, taking the photograph out of the envelope with a flourish and placing it in Mr. Marmalade's paw.

"Peru!" cried Mr. Marmalade. "You have every reason to be excited, for this is indeed a very good photograph of Matilda. Peru!" he cried again, as he peered more closely at the photograph, "that kitten doll is very like a kitten I once knew a long time ago; in fact it is very like me when *I* was a kitten!"

"Yes, indeed!" cried Mr. Smile Please Tom, "Mr. Jolly Jumbo Tom, the toy-making cat, made it exactly like you as a kitten."

"Peru!" purred Mr. Marmalade, "I think that Mr. Jolly Jumbo Tom is a *very* clever cat."

"This photograph has suddenly given me an idea!" cried Mr. Smile Please Tom. "I'll have a Happy Snaps Competition to help raise the money you need to buy *The Marigold Line.*"

"A wonderful idea," said Mr. Marmalade.

"I'll put a notice about it in *The Catville News* and *The Catville Times* straight away," said Mr. Smile Please Tom.

On his way to the newspaper offices, Mr. Smile Please Tom met his friend, Mr. Ali Baba, the Proud Persian.

"Hallo, there! You are the very cat I wanted to see," said Mr. Ali Baba. "I was just about to come round to your shop to buy a roll of film for my camera, but there's no hurry about that as I can get it another time. I *really* wanted to ask you if you had any bright ideas to help raise more money for *The Marigold Line*?"

Mr. Smile Please Tom's whiskers began to twitch and his green eyes twinkled. "Yes!" he cried, "a bright idea came to me when I was talking to Mr. Marmalade a few minutes ago. I'll tell you all about it."

Mr. Ali Baba pricked up his furry ears and listened carefully to every word that Mr. Smile Please Tom had to say about the Happy Snaps Competition. "I think it is a simply wonderful idea!" he cried, "and I hope it brings in lots and lots of silver shillings and sixpences."

When the newspaper reading cats opened their papers next morning, there, in the middle of the front page, was Mr. Smile Please Tom's notice, and this is what it said: "Get your cameras out and TAKE A HAPPY SNAP! Mr. Smile Please Tom will give prizes for the photos he likes best. Send YOUR snaps, together with one silver shilling entrance fee for big snaps and one silver sixpence for smaller snaps, to Mr. Smile Please Tom. All the competition entry money will be given to Mr. Marmalade to help him buy *The Marigold Line*."

When Mr. Black Tom read the notice in his paper, he promptly took a picture of Smoky, his errand-kitten. It showed him wearing a clean blue and white striped apron tied round his furry middle and holding a herring in his mouth. Mr. Marmalade also got out his camera and standing very still in front of his full-length looking-glass and, looking straight at his image in the mirror, he took a photograph of himself *taking a photograph of himself!*

A few days later, when the other cats had sent in their photographs, Mr. Smile Please Tom looked carefully through them and selected the ones he liked best. He then put another notice in the newspapers, this time giving the winners of the competition. It said, "WINNERS OF THE HAPPY SNAPS COMPETITION:

1. Miss Shani, the Siamese, wins a roll of colour film for taking a photo of Miss Tilly Tortoiseshell, wearing the prettiest hat.

2. Miss Tilly Tortoiseshell wins a roll of black and white film for taking a photo of Miss Shani, the Siamese, the prettiest lady cat from Foreign Parts.

3. Mr. Black Tom wins a photograph album for his amusing picture of Smoky.

4. Mr. Marmalade wins a brand-new camera for taking the *very* funniest picture."

After the prizes had been presented, Mr. Marmalade invited Mr. Smile Please Tom and all the winners to tea in the milk bar. Mr. Smile Please Tom set to work to count

*Mr. Marmalade stood very still before the looking-glass.*

all the silver shillings and sixpences and he found that he had enough silver sixpences to fill the sack in the fish shop, but, alas, nothing like enough silver shillings to fill the sack in the milk bar.

As soon as the sack of silver sixpences was filled, Mr. Black Tom slung it over his furry shoulder and carried it to the milk bar and placed it beside the shining black Wellington boot that was brim-full with copper pennies.

"Now we must put our furry heads together once more and try to think of another way to fill the other sack until it is simply bulging with silver shillings," said Mr. Black Tom.

"Peru!" said Mr. Marmalade, "I quite agree. But we haven't got too much time left to raise the money before Mr. Count-The-Pennies Tom closes *The Marigold Line* on July the 10th."

"What date is it now?" asked Mr. Black Tom.

"June the 30th," said Mr. Marmalade, "and that leaves us just ten whole days, which isn't very long."

"Oh, dear me, time really does fly!" cried

Mr. Black Tom. "Tell me again, just *when* is Mr. Count-The-Pennies Tom going to close *The Marigold Line*?"

"After the last train runs on July 10th," said Mr. Marmalade. "I only wish we knew a really wealthy cat!" he added, with a sigh.

"That would be wonderful," said Mr. Black Tom, "but as we don't know a really wealthy cat, we'll just have to put our furry heads together again and think very hard indeed."

## 7   *What the gipsy said*

The milk bar was very quiet as the two friends sat thinking. On the wall the hands of the cuckoo clock were slowly but surely creeping nearer and nearer to eleven as the clock tick-tocked the minutes away. Then, just as the cuckoo in the clock cuckooed eleven times, the door of the milk bar was pushed open and a gipsy cat, wearing gold ear-rings in her furry ears, entered and trotted briskly up to the counter. She was carrying a basket full of clothes-pegs, white clockwork mice for kittens, shoe laces, matches, whisker-curling pins, and packets of cat food.

Mr. Black Tom stopped thinking, politely jumped off his stool and gave a little bow to the gipsy cat. He took her basket and placed it on a small table by the counter then helped her to sit down on a high stool.

"I've been walking about Catville all morning selling my wares and I'm now very, very thirsty," said the gipsy cat.

"Peru!" said Mr. Marmalade, "I'm sure you are, ma'am. Walking always makes one thirsty."

"It does, indeed," said the gipsy cat.

"Well, then," said Mr. Marmalade, taking an extra large saucer off the shelf, "I'll give you a very big saucer of rich creamy milk."

"Thank you, kind sir," said the gipsy cat.

Mr. Marmalade took the shining red top off a fresh bottle of milk and filled the extra large saucer to the brim. For the next few minutes nothing could be heard except the tick-tocking of the cuckoo clock and the sound of the gipsy cat lapping up the milk. When she had finished, Mr. Marmalade filled the saucer to the brim again and soon she had lapped up every drop and licked the saucer quite clean for a second time.

"Thank you, kind sir," said the gipsy cat. "Now let me look at your paw and I'll tell your fortune."

Mr. Marmalade held out his right paw and

the gipsy cat looked at it very closely. "You are going to have a very wonderful surprise!" she said.

"Peru!" said Mr. Marmalade. "I wonder what it will be?"

"You'll know that when it happens, sir," said the gipsy cat.

"Please tell *my* fortune too!" said Mr. Black Tom, holding out his paw.

When she had looked at it very closely, she said, "You are going to have a very wonderful surprise, too!"

"What will it be?" asked Mr. Black Tom.

"The very same wonderful surprise that Mr. Marmalade is going to have," replied the gipsy cat.

At that moment, the cuckoo in the cuckoo clock cuckooed twice, and the gipsy cat stood up. "It is half-past eleven, and I must be going," she said, slipping the basket over her furry arm. "Thank you, kind sirs, and good day and good fortune to you both." She trotted briskly to the door and in a few moments was gone.

"Peru!" said Mr. Marmalade, "I wish I

knew what the very wonderful surprise was going to be!"

"So do I," said his friend. "But mind you, if we *did* know, then it wouldn't be a surprise, would it?"

"No, I suppose it wouldn't," agreed Mr. Marmalade.

The door opened again, and this time, Mr. Marmalade's sister, Toffee, trotted into the milk bar. She was wearing a new olive-green hat on her furry head and carried a new olive-green bag over her furry arm. "Hallo, Orange! Hallo, Mr. Black Tom!" she cried.

"Hallo, Toffee," said Mr. Marmalade.

"Delighted to see you," said Mr. Black Tom, standing up and bowing very low. "May I have the pleasure of helping you to sit down on one of Mr. Marmalade's high stools," he added politely.

"Thank you," she said. Mr. Black Tom held her arm while she sat down, then sat down again himself.

"Here is a saucer of rich creamy milk for you, dear sister," said Mr. Marmalade, carefully pushing the saucer across the counter.

"Thank you, dear furry brother," said Toffee, and when she had lapped up every drop, she said, "I'm very excited to-day!"

"Peru!" said Mr. Marmalade, "and why are you very excited?"

"Because I've just had a telegram from Micky," she said.

"From Micky!" gasped Mr. Marmalade, "but I thought he was still at sea?"

"So he is," said Toffee, "but he sent me a telegram by wireless to say that his ship, the S.S. *Felix*, will be arriving back at Fish Bay any time now. He also told me to tell you that he'd send *you* a telegram as soon as he knows when the ship is going to dock."

"I wonder why he wants to send *me* a telegram?" said Mr. Marmalade.

"I've no idea," said Toffee.

While Toffee was speaking, Teddy, the telegraph cat, brought his spluttering pillar-box red motor scooter to a stop outside the milk bar. A moment later, he trotted briskly into the shop and thrust a yellow envelope into Mr. Marmalade's outstretched paw. "A telegram for you, Mr. Marmalade," said Teddy.

"Thank you, Teddy," said Mr. Marmalade, tearing open the yellow envelope. He pulled out the telegram on which was printed in block letters: "THE S.S. FELIX DOCKS AT FISH BAY TO-MORROW. THERE IS A VERY IMPORTANT TRAVELLING CAT ON BOARD AND HE IS COMING TO CATVILLE WITH ME. HOPE YOU CAN PUT US UP. PLEASE MEET THE BOAT TRAIN WHICH ARRIVES AT 5 O'CLOCK (TO-MORROW)." It was signed "MICKY".

"Peru!" said Mr. Marmalade, "it looks as if the gipsy cat was right."

"What gipsy cat?" asked Toffee.

"There was a gispy cat in here shortly before you came in," answered Mr. Black Tom. "She said that Mr. Marmalade and I were going to have a very wonderful surprise."

"Oh, I see," said Toffee.

"Will you come with me to the station to-morrow, Toffee, and you too, Mr. Black Tom?" said Mr. Marmalade.

"Yes, *I'll* come!" cried Toffee. "My friend

Miss Prudence Persian, will look after the kitten shop while I'm away."

"Smoky can look after my fish shop," said Mr. Black Tom.

"And Mrs. Stripy's kitten, Suzy, can look after the milk bar," said Mr. Marmalade.

"Please, Mr. Marmalade, may *I* come too?" said Miss Tilly Tortoiseshell, who had been standing quietly in the doorway for the last few minutes.

"Peru!" purred Mr. Marmalade, "I'd be delighted if you would come."

"Thank you," said Miss Tilly Tortoiseshell, and added that Geraldine, her old school friend, would surely look after the mitten shop for her while she was out.

"Then that's settled," said Mr. Black Tom.

"Now I'd better help you to get a bed ready for Micky and another bed for the very important travelling cat," said Toffee, and she trotted round the counter and through the door into the little sitting room behind the shop.

"I'll help, too," said Miss Tilly Tortoise-shell, trotting after her.

"Thank you both very much indeed," said Mr. Marmalade, politely. "*I'd* better be getting back to the fish shop or Smoky will be wondering where I've got to," said Mr. Black Tom. "See you soon!"

"See you at the station to-morrow," said Mr. Marmalade, waving his paw.

Mr. Marmalade sat down and wondered who it was that Micky was bringing home with him to Catville. But though he thought and thought, he just could not think who it could be.

Micky Marmalade was Mr. Marmalade's young brother, and very nearly as handsome as Mr. Marmalade himself. When he left school shortly before last Christmas, Micky had told Mr. Marmalade that he wanted more than anything else to go to sea and be a sailing cat.

"Please, Orange," Micky had said, "do you think your friend, Mr. Jack Tar Tom, the ship-owning cat, will let me join one of his ships?"

"Peru!" Mr. Marmalade had replied, "I don't know, but I'll go and ask him if you like, and you'd better come with me."

So it was that the very next day, Mr. Taxi-Driver Tom whisked Mr. Marmalade and a very excited Micky to the station where they caught the express train to Fish Bay. Mr. Jack Tar Tom had met them at Fish Bay station and, after they had greeted each other and wished each other a very happy Christmas —for don't forget it *was* Christmas time—Mr. Jack Tar Tom whisked them away in his big shining black motor car to his house, Cod Fish Mansion. This was a big white stone house high up on the headland which jutted out into the deep blue sea.

Mr. Jack Tar Tom listened while Micky explained why he wanted to go to sea and be a sailing cat, and he promised that he would think about it. "Now you must both stay with me for Christmas," he had added.

While Micky was down at the jetty looking at all the tugs and barges, dredgers, ferry and cargo boats, Mr. Jack Tar Tom had winked one of his big green eyes at Mr. Marmalade and said, "I think I'll be able to fix him up on one of my ships very soon, but not a word to young Micky, mind! Let it be a real surprise."

As soon as Mr. Marmalade had heard this, he had picked up the telephone and dialled CAT 222. This was his sister's number, and when she came on the phone a moment later, he told her that Micky would be sailing very soon.

"*I'll* tell Miss Tilly Tortoiseshell and Mr. Black Tom," said Toffee, "for I'm quite sure they'll like to know."

The next day, with help from Mr. Marmalade and Micky, Mr. Jack Tar Tom had decorated Cod Fish Mansion with gay paper streamers and sprigs of mistletoe, ivy and holly. A bushy little Christmas tree had been decorated with red, gold, green and blue glass balls and sparkling silver tinsel. While they were doing this, Mr. Jack Tar Tom's wife, Hazel, had baked a Christmas cake and put pink sugar icing on top, and Mr. Jack Tar Tom's daughter, Constance, had made some delicious mince pies.

The day after that, when Micky was once more down at the jetty looking at the ships, Mr. Marmalade had gone into the town to do some Christmas shopping. Later that very same day, a little sea-green motor van, driven by Mr. Carrier Tom, had rumbled to a stop outside Cod Fish Mansion, and Mr. Carrier Tom delivered some bulky parcels. Three of the parcels had come from Catville and they were all addressed to Micky Marmalade. The fourth parcel, which was also addressed to Micky and very bulky indeed, was from Mr. Marmalade, who had bought it in the town that very morning.

When Micky set eyes on the parcels, he had wanted to open them straight away, but he didn't do so because on each one was stuck a holly-berry red label on which was written in red ink, "NOT TO BE OPENED UNTIL CHRIST-MAS DAY."

On Christmas morning, after they had wished each other a Happy Christmas and opened their Christmas cards, Micky opened his parcels. The first one, wrapped in bright red paper, was from Mr. Black Tom, and Micky was delighted to find that it contained a brand-new navy blue sailor suit with shining brass buttons and a white peaked cap. In the second parcel, he found a sou'wester and a pair of sea-boots from his sister, Toffee, and in the third parcel (which wasn't quite as bulky as the others) he found two pairs of navy blue mittens. These came from Miss Tilly Tortoiseshell. When he took the wrapping off the last and biggest parcel of all, he found a big wooden sea-chest in which he could keep all his favourite tins of cat food and sweet milk! This present was from Mr. Marmalade.

"Thank you!" Micky had cried, "now I've got everything a sailing cat needs, except a ship!"

"And you've got that, too!" cried Mr. Jack Tar Tom, who had been watching Micky opening his presents. "You can join my biggest ship, the S.S. *Felix*, which sails out of Fish Bay on the day after Boxing Day for a trip round the world!"

"Oh, thank you, sir," Micky had cried. "That is the most exciting Christmas present I've ever had!"

"You'll start as a cadet-cat," Mr. Jack Tar Tom had said, "and when you know all there is to know about ships and sailors, the stars and the compass and how to steer a ship north, south, east or west, I'll make you a Captain, Micky. One day you'll be in command of a big ship of your very own!"

Mr. Marmalade remembered the day after Boxing Day very clearly, for that was the day that Mr. Carrier Tom came in his little sea-green motor van and took Micky's luggage to the jetty where the S.S. *Felix* was tied up. Mr. Marmalade also remembered standing on the jetty to wave good-bye to Micky, who looked very handsome indeed in his new sailor suit.

Mr. Marmalade had not seen Micky since then, though he had had picture post-cards from him when the ship called at Australia and New York.

Now he was coming home again . . .

## 8  *Surprise at the station*

Mr. Marmalade was so excited he could hardly sleep a wink that night, and the next afternoon he popped his straw hat on his furry head, and trotted out of the shop, not stopping until he was on Platform 4 of the railway station. Within a few minutes, his sister, Toffee, Miss Tilly Tortoiseshell, and Mr. Black Tom trotted along the platform and stood beside him.

"It's five minutes to five," said Mr. Black Tom, looking at the station clock, "so we've only five minutes to wait."

"I'm very excited," said Toffee.

"So am I," said Miss Tilly Tortoiseshell.

"Peru! And so am *I*," said Mr. Marmalade.

The boat train did arrive at 5 o'clock, just as Micky had said it would.

"Peru!" cried Mr. Marmalade, waving his paw, "there's Micky coming out of a First Class carriage. He's with a jolly American-looking cat who is wearing a ten-gallon hat on his furry head and has *two* cameras slung over his shoulder."

"Hallo! Hallo! Micky," cried Mr. Marmalade. "Welcome home to Catville."

Toffee, who had been looking at the American-looking cat, suddenly cried, "Why, it's our uncle, Squire Marmalade! So this is the very important travelling cat!"

Micky grinned. "Yes," he said, "Uncle Marmalade is the very important travelling cat I told you to expect."

"Peru!" cried Mr. Marmalade, "welcome home to Catville, Uncle Marmalade!"

"Thank you, nephew," said Squire Marmalade. "I haven't seen my nephews and my niece since you were tiny kittens, and I must say you've grown into very handsome cats!"

After Mr. Marmalade had introduced Miss Tilly Tortoiseshell and Mr. Black Tom to Squire Marmalade, he said. "Now we'll all go home in Mr. Taxi-Driver Tom's daffodil-yellow taxi."

That evening, after tea, Mr. Marmalade and his uncle, Micky and Toffee and Mr.

*There was Micky with a jolly, American-looking cat.*

Black Tom and Miss Tilly Tortoiseshell sat for a long time in the little sitting room behind the shop.

"You seem to have done very well for yourself, nephew," said Squire Marmalade to Mr. Marmalade. "This is the cosiest milk bar I've ever seen and I've seen many in my time!"

"Peru!" said Mr. Marmalade, proudly, "it *is* a cosy milk bar and it is also a prosperous one because I sell only the richest and creamiest milk in Catville."

"All the rich creamy milk comes from Mr. Marmalade's farm, which is near Marmalade Mansion, Mr. Marmalade's country house," Mr. Black Tom explained.

"Yes," said Miss Tilly Tortoiseshell, "and that is very near Squire Marmalade's country house, Marmalade Manor. It is also on *The Marigold Line*, which Mr. Count-The-Pennies Tom is going to close unless we can raise enough money to buy it."

"Don't worry!" drawled Squire Marmalade. "That's just why I came back home to Catville. You see, when I switched on my wireless one day in New York and heard that *The Marigold Line* was going to be closed, I made up my mind to come right back and do something about it! Now, then, nephew," he said to Mr. Marmalade, "how much money do you need, eh?"

"Peru!" said Mr. Marmalade, "we have one shining black Wellington boot filled to the brim with copper pennies and one sack bulging with silver sixpences. But the sack for silver shillings is only about half full!"

"Then *I'll* fill it!" cried Squire Marmalade. Then and there, he trotted out of the little sitting room and up the stairs to the bedroom that Toffee and Miss Tilly Tortoiseshell had got ready for him. He opened the tin box that was filled to the brim with the fortune he had made in America, brought some bags of silver shillings out and carried them downstairs into the milk bar. "Now then, nephew," he said to Mr. Marmalade, "if you will hold open your sack for silver shillings, I'll fill it for you."

A few moments later, Squire Marmalade had filled the sack until it was simply bulging with silver shillings. "Now, there you are!" he cried, "You have all the money you need to buy *The Marigold Line!*"

"Peru!" cried Mr. Marmalade, "thank you, thank you, Uncle!"

"Well," drawled Squire Marmalade, who had quite an American accent, "I guess I've made my fortune in America all right, and there's not much point in making a fortune if you don't use it in a good cause!"

"And you came all the way back from America to Catville to save *The Marigold Line?*" said Toffee.

"Yes, I did," said Squire Marmalade, "and now that I'm here, I guess I'll go and live in Marmalade Manor for good now! I'm sure tired of being a fortune-hunting and travelling cat!"

"Come on!" cried Mr. Black Tom, "let's take all the money to Mr. Count-The-Pennies Tom. Just wait while I phone for a taxi."

While Mr. Black Tom was on the telephone, Squire Marmalade, who had been told about the Sunday School picnic, gave Mr. Marmalade two more bags of silver shillings.

*The silver shillings poured into the sack!*

"There'll be enough money there," he said, "for you to get *Puffing Pussy* and the coaches mended in time for Miss Shani, the Siamese, to take her class of kittens on their picnic."

"Peru!" cried Mr. Marmalade. "Thank you again, Uncle Marmalade, for all you have done."

"Don't mention it, my boy," said Squire Marmalade. "And now, while you are seeing Mr. Count-The-Pennies Tom, I'll sit back in your cosy armchair and read *The Catville News*. I haven't done that for a long, long time!" he chuckled.

A few seconds later, Mr. Taxi-Driver Tom drove up in his daffodil-yellow taxi-cab. Mr. Marmalade and Mr. Black Tom put the two sacks and the shining black Wellington boot into the taxi, and then Mr. Marmalade and Mr. Black Tom, Toffee and Miss Tilly Tortoiseshell, jumped into the taxi too. Mr. Taxi-Driver Tom started the engine and whisked them away to the station.

## 9  *Mr. Marmalade makes a purchase*

After Mr. Black Tom had paid Mr. Taxi-Driver Tom, he slung the sack of silver sixpences over his shoulder. Mr. Marmalade slung the sack of silver shillings over *his* shoulder, and Miss Tilly Tortoiseshell and Toffee carried the shining black Wellington boot between them.

They stopped when they came to the door marked "STRICTLY PRIVATE. This is the Office of Mr. Count-The-Pennies Tom, the General Manager and President of The Catville Railway Company. NO CAT MAY COME IN UNLESS ON VERY IMPORTANT BUSINESS INDEED."

"Peru!" said Mr. Marmalade, "I'm quite sure that *we* are on Very Important Business!"

"We certainly are!" cried Miss Tilly Tortoiseshell.

Mr. Marmalade pushed open the door and

they climbed up the steep and wobbly wooden staircase. At the top Mr. Marmalade pushed open another door and they all trotted into the long office with the high wooden desk and big shining window.

Mr. Count-The-Pennies Tom was sitting at his high wooden desk. When he saw Mr. Marmalade and his friends and the bulging sacks of silver shillings and sixpences and the copper pennies in the shining black Wellington boot, he cried, "So, you've come to buy *The Marigold Line*?"

"Peru!" cried Mr. Marmalade, dropping his sack to the floor. "We have indeed! And this sack is full of silver shillings."

"And *this* sack is full of silver sixpences!" cried Mr. Black Tom, dropping his sack to the floor.

"And this shining black Wellington boot is filled to the brim with copper pennies," said Toffee, as she and Miss Tilly Tortoiseshell placed it on the floor beside the two sacks.

"Well, then, *The Marigold Line* is yours from this very moment!" said Mr. Count-

The-Pennies Tom. "But wait a moment while I put it down in writing for you."

They waited quietly while Mr. Count-The-Pennies Tom wrote on a piece of clean white paper: The Marigold Line now belongs to Mr. Marmalade. Signed, Count-The-Pennies Tom.

"There you are," said Mr. Count-The-Pennies Tom, handing the paper to Mr. Marmalade. "And I hope that lots and lots of cats and kittens will travel on it."

Mr. Marmalade put the piece of paper in his pocket and then he invited Mr. Count-The-Pennies Tom to come on *The Marigold Special* on Tuesday, 20th July. Mr. Count-The-Pennies Tom was pleased to accept the invitation and before they left his office, he promised to lend them another engine and set of coaches to use on *The Marigold Line* while *Puffing Pussy* and its battered coaches were being mended.

"Now then," said Mr. Marmalade, when they were outside the station a few minutes later, "there are one or two things we must do straight away."

"What sort of things?" asked Toffee.

"Well, first we must tell Miss Shani, the Siamese, that she *can* take her class of thirty kittens on *The Marigold Special* for their picnic. Then we must see Mr. Sooty-Paws, the chimney-sweeping cat, and ask him to bring his long, bristly brushes and sweep the chimney of *Puffing Pussy*. Next we must see Roger, the railway engineering cat, and ask him to oil *Puffing Pussy's* wheels and get a new boiler for her and lastly, we must see Mr. Painter Tom and ask him to paint *Puffing Pussy* and all the coaches."

"*I'll* see Miss Shani, the Siamese," said Miss Tilly Tortoiseshell.

"And *I'll* see Mr. Sooty-Paws," said Toffee.

"And *I'll* see Roger," said Mr. Black Tom.

"Peru!" said Mr. Marmalade. "And *I'll* see Mr. Painter Tom."

"We'll go and see them straight away," said Mr. Black Tom.

When Miss Shani, the Siamese, heard the good news, she was so excited she danced a Special Siamese Dance and told Annette, her maid-kitten, that she would have an *extra* bath that day just to cool her down!

The next day, *Puffing Pussy* went into the engine shed. Roger, the railway-engineering cat, brought a brand-new boiler for her and oiled her wheels. Mr. Sooty-Paws swept her chimney with his long bristly brushes, and when that was done, Mr. Painter Tom painted her all over in bright red and gold paint. Mr. Artist Tom painted a picture of Mr. Marmalade's furry form, holding a marigold in his paw, on the very front of the engine, and the letters T M L (which meant *The Marigold Line*), he painted on either side of the driving cab.

As soon as *Puffing Pussy* was mended and oiled and painted, Roger and Mr. Painter Tom set to work on the coaches. Soon all the windows were clean again, the torn seats mended and covered with bright red and gold coverings and the outside of the coaches freshly painted to match the engine.

Meanwhile, Mr. Printer Tom had printed dozens and dozens of tickets. There were green tickets for First Class travelling cats, blue tickets for Second Class travelling cats and chocolate brown tickets for travelling kittens.

Next morning, when the newspaper-reading cats opened their papers, their attention was caught by a notice printed in the biggest black letters ever seen in Catville. It said: "MR. MARMALADE WISHES TO LET EVERY CAT AND KITTEN IN CATVILLE KNOW THAT, THANKS TO THE KIND GIFTS OF HIS FRIENDS AND HIS RICH UNCLE, SQUIRE MARMALADE, HE NOW OWNS THE MARIGOLD LINE. *Puffing Pussy* and the battered old coaches are now mended and painted in fresh colours and will run again on Tuesday, 20th July." The notice was signed: "ORANGE, MR. MARMALADE."

When all the newspaper-reading cats heard that Mr. Marmalade now owned *The Marigold Line*, there was tremendous excitement in Catville, and on the morning of 20th July, dozens and dozens of cats and kittens queued up at the booking office to buy their tickets. It was a warm, sunny morning, and Mr. Weatherwise Tom had told Mr. Marmalade that he was quite sure it was going to be a warm, sunny day as well.

At nine o'clock, Miss Shani, the Siamese, trotted into the crowded station, her class of thirty Sunday School kittens (each carrying packets of fish-paste sandwiches), walking two by two behind her. As she led them towards the booking office, Mr. Marmalade came up to her. Sweeping off his hat and bowing low, he said, "Peru! *You* don't need to buy any tickets. Now that I own *The Marigold Line*, I've made up my mind that you and your kittens can travel quite free!"

"Oh, thank you, Mr. Marmalade," said Miss Shani, the Siamese.

"*I* will show you to your seats," said Mr. Ali Baba, the Proud Persian. "Please follow me." Miss Shani and her class of thirty kittens trotted along the platform after Mr. Ali Baba. "Here you are," said Mr. Ali Baba, opening the door of a First Class carriage. "You'll have this coach all to yourselves."

"What comfortable seats," said Miss Shani, sitting down with her back to the engine.

"I think we are all going to enjoy our day out in the country."

At five minutes past nine, Mr. Black Tom and Smoky trotted along the platform to their seats in the train. Five minutes later, Miss Tilly Tortoiseshell, Toffee and Micky Marmalade joined Mr. Marmalade in his compartment. At twenty minutes past nine, Mr. MacPherson Tom and Mr. Mackintosh, the wild cat, arrived with their bagpipes. Their singing friend, Mr. Daffadowndilly Tom, the Welsh cat, joined them. Then at twenty-five minutes past nine all the cats and kittens who had helped to raise money to save *The Marigold Line* trotted along the platform and took their seats in *The Marigold Special*. Last but not least, came Mr. Count-The-Pennies Tom, who climbed into the train and sat beside Mr. Marmalade.

"If only I had thought of painting the engine and carriages, and oiling the wheels and mending the boiler, this train would have been as full of travelling cats and kittens as it is to-day," said Mr. Count-The-Pennies Tom.

"Peru!" said Mr. Marmalade, "I'm quite

sure you *would* have thought of doing all those things had you not been so very busy thinking about all the express trains that run on the *main* lines!" Mr. Marmalade leaned over and whispered in Mr. Count-The-Pennies Tom's ear, "What *you* need is an assistant cat to help you!" he said.

"You're quite right!" cried Mr. Count-The-Pennies Tom. "I *am* a very busy cat. I'll do as you say and get an assistant cat to help me and then I shan't need to close any more branch lines because I'm too busy to run them properly!"

As the hands on the station clock moved nearer and nearer to half-past nine, the lady announcing-cat began to speak over the station loud-speaker: "The red and gold train now standing at Platform One is *The Marigold Special*, and the pretty branch line on which it runs is to be called *The Marigold Line*. *The Marigold Special* will leave Catville this morning and EVERY morning (except Sunday) for Marmalade Manor, at half-past nine. It will call at Whisker Junction, Marmalade Mansion Halt, Thistle Junction, Marmalade

Farm, Buttercup Halt, Daisy Meadow, Dandelion Point, Daffodil Corner (Low Level), and, of course, Marmalade Manor for Marigold Lane—the perfect place for Picnics."

A few seconds later, at half-past nine exactly, the guard waved his green flag and blew a shrill blast on his whistle. With a hoot and a toot from the engine and a hiss of steam, Mr. Engine-Driver Tom drove *Puffing Pussy* and the train out of the station.

They arrived at Marmalade Manor exactly on time, and there, standing on the platform waiting to welcome them, was Squire Marmalade himself, looking for all the world like a cowboy cat with his big ten-gallon hat.

"Welcome, folks. Welcome to Marmalade Manor," said Squire Marmalade. "I only moved in yesterday and the place needs tidying up, but I guess you folks won't mind that!" To Miss Shani, the Siamese, and her class of kittens he said, "Have a happy day picnicking in Marigold Lane, and don't forget to call at Marmalade Manor where there'll be a bottle of fizzy pop for each kitten!"

"Peru!" cried Mr. Marmalade. "I think that *I'll* call for a bottle of fizzy pop, too!"

"So will I," said Mr. Black Tom.

And so they all did—even Mr. Count-The-Pennies Tom, who had not drunk fizzy pop since he was a kitten. Then they trotted along Marigold Lane to the picnic field, where the kittens played Hide and Seek and chased each other's furry tails. Mr. Marmalade and his friends and all the other grown-up cats played Hide and Seek and chased each other's furry tails, too!

"Peru!" said Mr. Marmalade. "I always knew that we cats were really kittens at heart!"

Miss Black Whiskers kept the tiny village shop that stood in the shade of a giant oak tree at the corner of Marigold Lane. She was a very old lady cat with stripes like a tiger and she wore a red velvet collar with a tinkling bell round her furry neck. When Squire Marmalade had called that morning to tell her that he was going to live at Marmalade Manor for good, she was very pleased. He told her that he was going to buy from her all his tins of salmon, sardines, pilchards, meat and sweet milk (he had a *very* sweet tooth), butter and cheese, plus paraffin oil for his oil lamps and heaters, wax candles and boxes of matches and many many more things besides. She was really delighted, and later

*"Welcome, folks. Welcome to Marmalade Manor!"*

when she saw Mr. Marmalade and his friends, and Miss Shani, the Siamese, and her class of thirty happy kittens come trotting along the lane, she was quite overjoyed. You see, while Squire Marmalade had been away in America making his fortune, Marmalade Manor had been empty. Until Mr. Marmalade had bought *The Marigold Line* very few cats or kittens had come to her tiny shop, and, truth to tell, she had taken so few pennies, silver sixpences and shillings that she hardly made enough money to pay herself any wages! Now that Squire Marmalade was going to buy all his groceries from her, she would, at last, be able to pay herself some wages again. She was also quite sure that the picnicking cats would now come into her shop for fizzy pop and ice-cream and catmint rock. And, of course, she was quite right. They *did* squeeze into her tiny shop to spend their copper pennies and silver sixpences and shillings on biscuits and sweets, fizzy pop and ice-cream and catmint rock!

"Peru!" cried Mr. Marmalade, when he went into the shop. "I think I'll send a picture post-card to my cousin Arabella." Pushing the picture post-card stand lightly, he sent it whirling round, and when it stopped, he saw the very picture post-card that he wanted. "Peru!" he cried, taking the post-card from the stand. "I'll have this picture of Marmalade Manor, if you please."

"Thank you, Mr. Marmalade," said Miss Black Whiskers. "That will be three copper pennies, please."

Mr. Marmalade took three pennies from his pocket and gave them to Miss Black Whiskers. He also bought a stamp which he stuck on the card, and borrowing a pen from Miss Black Whiskers (for he'd left his own pen at home), he dipped it in the ink-pot and wrote, "I wish you were here!—Orange." When he had written Arabella's name and address, he popped the card into the letter box.

"*I'll* send *this* card to my friend, Mr. Lighthouse-Keeper Tom and his wife, Belinda, at Catmint-on-Sea," said Mr. Black Tom, choosing a picture of *Puffing Pussy* looking spick and span in her new paint. This was a brand-new picture taken by Mr. Smile Please Tom only yesterday! Mr. Black Tom wrote on *his* card, "I wish *you* were here, too," and he signed it, "Jolly Black Tom."

Then Mr. Marmalade bought some sticks of catmint rock for Miss Shani's happy kittens, and when no one was looking, he bought a stick for himself!

After the kittens had played their games, and after the grown-up cats had played *their* games, Mr. MacPherson Tom played his bagpipes while Mr. Mackintosh danced a Scottish dance. Then their friend, Mr. Daffa-downdilly Tom, the Welsh cat, sang a song. How the cats and kittens clapped their furry paws.

"And now *I* have a surprise for the happy kittens!" cried Mr. Jolly Jumbo Tom, the toy-making cat. He opened the lid of a wooden box and brought out thirty tiny models of *Puffing Pussy*. Each was painted in red and gold and had a picture of Mr. Marmalade—holding a marigold—on the front just like the *real Puffing Pussy*. "I made these models myself!" he cried. "And I'm now going to give one to each of Miss Shani's happy kittens!"

The kittens were delighted with their lovely models of *Puffing Pussy* and they thanked Mr. Jumbo Tom very politely.

"Peru!" cried Mr. Marmalade. "*I* have a surprise for you, too! All of my friends can have FREE SAUCERS OF RICH CREAMY MILK IN THE MARMALADE MILK BAR as often as you like during the next few weeks, because, if YOU hadn't given me so many copper pennies and so many silver sixpences and so many silver shillings, I would not have been able to buy *The Marigold Line* from Mr. Count-The-Pennies Tom."

"Three cheers for Mr. Marmalade!" cried Miss Tilly Tortoiseshell, "Hip-hip!"

"Hoo-ray!" cried the cats and happy kittens. "Hip-hip!"

"Hoo-ray!" cried the cats and happy kittens again.

"Hip-hip!"

"Hoo-ray!" cried the cats and happy kittens for the third time.

The picnic was now almost over and everyone was getting ready to catch *The Marigold Special* back to Catville. Miss Shani, the Siamese, thanked Mr. Marmalade and his friends for all they had done to give them one of the happiest days they had ever had. "We'll all come picnicking to Marmalade Manor and Marigold Lane again!" she purred.

"And again and again and *again!*" cried the happy kittens.

"Peru! And so will we!" cried Mr. Marmalade. And of course, they *did*!

**THE END**